EUROPEAN COUNTRIES TODAY
NETHERLANDS

EUROPEAN COUNTRIES TODAY

TITLES IN THE SERIES

EUROPEAN COUNTRIES TODAY
NETHERLANDS

Dominic J. Ainsley

MASON CREST

Mason Crest
450 Parkway Drive, Suite D
Broomall, Pennsylvania PA 19008
(866) MCP-BOOK (toll free)

First printing
9 8 7 6 5 4 3 2 1

ISBN: 978-1-4222-3988-9
Series ISBN: 978-1-4222-3977-3
ebook ISBN: 978-1-4222-7803-1

Cataloging-in-Publication Data on file with the Library of Congress.

Printed in the United States of America

Cover images
Main: *Amsterdam.*
Left: *A Dutch fish market.*
Center: *A tulip farm in the northern Netherlands.*
Right: *The cheese market in Gouda.*

QR CODES AND LINKS TO THIRD-PARTY CONTENT

CONTENTS

KEY ICONS TO LOOK FOR:

Words to Understand: These words with their easy-to-understand definitions will increase the reader's understanding of the text while building vocabulary skills.

Sidebars: This boxed material within the main text allows readers to build knowledge, gain insights, explore possibilities, and broaden their perspectives by weaving together additional information to provide realistic and holistic perspectives.

Educational Videos: Readers can view videos by scanning our QR codes, providing them with additional content to supplement the text. Examples include news coverage, moments in history, speeches, iconic sports moments, and much more!

Text-Dependent Questions: These questions send the reader back to the text for more careful attention to the evidence presented there.

Research Projects: Readers are pointed toward areas of further inquiry connected to each chapter. Suggestions are provided for projects that encourage deeper research and analysis.

THE NETHERLANDS AT A GLANCE

MAP OF EUROPE

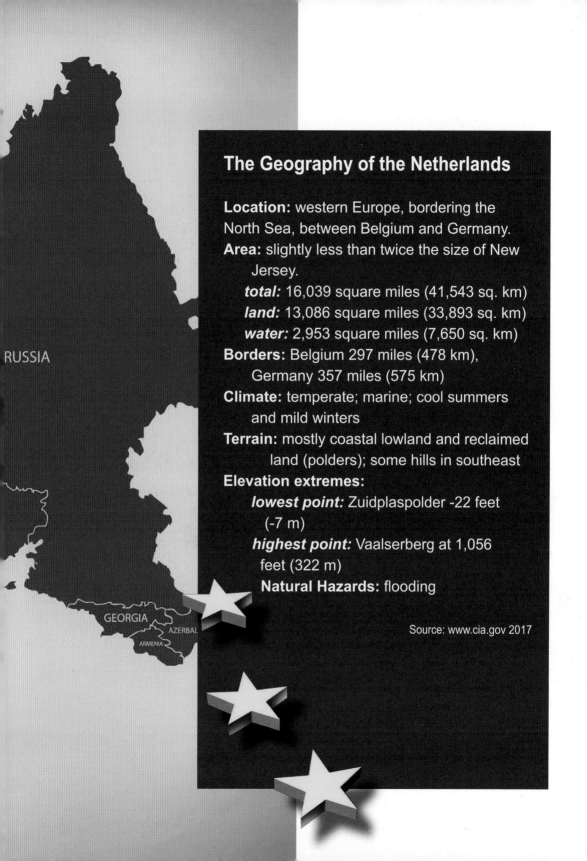

The Geography of the Netherlands

Location: western Europe, bordering the North Sea, between Belgium and Germany.

Area: slightly less than twice the size of New Jersey.

   total: 16,039 square miles (41,543 sq. km)

   land: 13,086 square miles (33,893 sq. km)

   water: 2,953 square miles (7,650 sq. km)

Borders: Belgium 297 miles (478 km), Germany 357 miles (575 km)

Climate: temperate; marine; cool summers and mild winters

Terrain: mostly coastal lowland and reclaimed land (polders); some hills in southeast

Elevation extremes:

   lowest point: Zuidplaspolder -22 feet (-7 m)

   highest point: Vaalserberg at 1,056 feet (322 m)

   Natural Hazards: flooding

Source: www.cia.gov 2017

Flag of the Netherlands

The Netherlands is a low-lying country in northern Europe. It is a highly populated country, two-fifths of which lies below sea level, making it susceptible to flooding. Large areas have been reclaimed from the sea, and for centuries inundation has been prevented by the construction of dykes and sand dunes along the coast.

The flag dates back to 1630, when it was first adopted, and is one of the oldest flags in Europe. At the end of the sixteenth century, the Netherlands was part of the Spanish Empire. The fight for independence was led by Prince William of Orange, of the House of Nassau-Dillenburg, who was assassinated by a Roman Catholic in 1584. The first flag was based on his livery.

ABOVE: The outdoor cafés and bars are a familiar sight beside the canals of Amsterdam, the capital city of the Netherlands.

The People of the Netherlands

Population: 17,084,719

Ethnic groups: Dutch, Turkish, Indonesian, Moroccan

Age structure:

0–14 years 16.41%

15–64 years 64.86%

65 years and above 18.73%

Population grown rate: 0.39%

Birth rate: 10.9 births/1,000 pop.

Death rate: 8.9 deaths/1,000 pop.

Migration rate: 1.9 migrants/1,000 pop.

Infant mortality rate: 3.6 deaths/1,000 live births

Life expectancy at birth:

Total population: 81.4 years

Male: 79.3 years

Female: 83.7 years

Total fertility rate: 1.78 children born/woman

Religions: Roman Catholic 28%, Protestant 19% (includes Dutch Reformed 9%, Protestant Church of the Netherlands 7%, Calvinist 3%), other 11% (includes about 5% Muslim and smaller numbers of Hindu, Buddhist, Jehovah's Witness, and Orthodox), none 42%

Languages: Dutch (official), Frisian (official)

Literacy rate: 99%

Source: www.cia.gov 2017

Words to Understand

dams: Barriers (as across streams) to hold back flows of water.

dikes: Mounds of earth built to control water.

sand dunes: Hills of sand.

BELOW: The famous Kinderdijk windmills are situated in the Alblasserwaard polder in the province of South Holland. They were originally used to pump excess water from the polders. The windmills were granted UNESCO World Heritage status in 1997.

Chapter One
THE NETHERLANDS' GEOGRAPHY & LANDSCAPE

The Netherlands, like the name suggests, is a low-lying country. About half of the country's territory lies no more than three feet (1 meter) above sea level, and one-fourth of the country is below sea level. **Dikes**, canals, **dams**, sluices, and windmills are distinctive features of the Dutch landscape. They are a critical part of the extensive water-drainage system that has enabled the Dutch to expand their country's land by almost one-fifth. More importantly, without this constant drainage and the protection of dunes along the nation's coast, almost half of the Netherlands would be flooded—mainly by the sea, but also by the many rivers that cross it. Canals, rivers, and coastal inlets cut through much of the low-lying western part of the country. Farther to the east, the land lies slightly higher and is flat or gently rolling. The elevation rarely exceeds 160 feet (50 meters). Most of the land is devoted to agriculture.

The total area of the Netherlands is slightly larger than the states of Massachusetts, Connecticut, and Rhode Island combined. At its widest point from east to west the Netherlands extends 120 miles (193 kilometers), and from north to south the greatest distance is 190 miles (306 kilometers).

ABOVE: *Rotterdam is a major European port that handles millions of shipping containers each year.*

Educational Video

This video provides a brief insight into the Netherlands' geography. Scan the QR code with your phone to watch!

ABOVE: *A typical Dutch polder. The farmland is drained using a series of ditches and pumps.*

ABOVE: *The island of Ameland in Friesland is part of the Wadden Islands archipelago, a scattered group of islands along the North Sea coast of the Netherlands.*

The Netherlands is bordered on the east by Germany, on the south by Belgium, and on the north and west by the North Sea. The coastline of the North Sea consists mostly of **sand dunes**. Many of the country's major cities are located on these slightly elevated dunes. In the north, the sea has broken through the dunes to form the West Frisian Islands.

Dike, Dams, and Polder Land

In the south, rivers have broken through the dunes and created a delta of islands and waterways. Near the narrow strip of dunes is a low-lying area protected by dikes and kept dry by continuous mechanical pumping. This is

Tulip

Tulip is the common name for thousands of varieties of flowers produced from bulbs comprising the genus *Tulipa*. They are valued for their brilliant colors and shapes. Cultivars include single color, striped, variegated, feathered, and flamed. Grown all over the world, tulips are a familiar sight in our gardens and widely associated with spring. For centuries the tulip has been synonymous with the Netherlands and fields of tulips are still a common sight in the country. However, the flowers actually originated in Persia. It is unclear how tulips arrived in northwest Europe, but it is believed that they were brought to the Netherlands by Ogier Ghislain de Busbecq in 1554.

polder land that the Dutch have reclaimed from the sea and turned into productive farmland. Dikes were built around sections of swampy or flooded land and water was pumped out, at first by windmills and later by steam and electric pumps. Reinforcing dikes were also built along the lower sections of the Netherlands' major rivers, which flow above the land between the banks of sediment deposited when they flood.

The Dutch began efforts to reclaim the Zuider Zee, a large segment of land covered by the North Sea, in 1927. By 1932, a large dike had been built across the entrance of the Zuider Zee. The dike turned the water behind it into a freshwater lake within five years. By the early 1980s, about three-quarters of the area had been drained, but the project to reclaim the last polder was canceled in the early 1980s. The freshwater lake left behind is called

Ijsselmeer. In 1953, a spring tide severely flooded the delta region on the southwest, and almost two thousand people died. The Delta Plan, launched in 1958 and completed in 1986, was implemented to prevent such flooding from happening again.

Under the plan the Dutch shortened their coastline by 435 miles (about 700 kilometers) and developed a system of dikes. They also built dams, bridges, locks, and a major canal. The dikes created freshwater lakes and joined some islands. The polders are used almost exclusively for agriculture and are

ABOVE: *The small fishing village of Urk is next to Ijsselmeer (a large freshwater lake that has been dammed off from the North Sea).*

ABOVE: *The view from Vaalserberg Hill. The photograph shows the Drielanden Labyrinth (or Three-Country Labyrinth), which is the largest shrub maze in Europe. The hill marks the spot where the Netherlands, Belgium, and Germany meet.*

comprised chiefly of clay, soils, and peat. Most of the eastern part of the Netherlands is covered by sandy soil deposited by glaciers, wind, and rivers. The nation's only hills are the foothills of the Ardennes. These hills with their fertile loamy soil are found only in the southern part of Limburg Province, an area of rich farmland. Vaalserberg, the nation's highest point is in this area.

Sixty percent of the nation's population currently lives at or below sea level, making the Netherlands particularly vulnerable to any rise in sea level induced by the greenhouse effect. As a result, the Dutch have been at the forefront of calls to reduce the dependency on fossil fuels and to bring deforestation to a halt. The Netherlands contributes less than 1 percent of global greenhouse emissions. Dutch agriculture depends heavily on the use of fertilizer, and significant nitrate pollution has occurred in water. In addition, pigs and other livestock produce large amounts of manure and ammonium gas, polluting ground water resources and affecting vegetation. The government has implemented new policies that require farmers to process manure in ways that are environmentally sound.

Climate

The Netherlands enjoys the temperate maritime climate that is found across much of northern and western Europe. Winds from the North Sea give the Netherlands mild winters and cool summers. Cloudless skies are uncommon, as is prolonged frost. Because the Netherlands has few natural barriers such as high mountains, the climate varies little from region to region.

ABOVE: *The Nederrijn is the name given to the Dutch section of the river Rhine. This photograph was taken near Arnhem.*

Rivers and Lakes

The major rivers of the Netherlands are the Rhine, flowing from Germany, and its several tributaries, like the Waal and Nederrijn rivers. Other important waterways include the Maas and the Schelde, which originate in Belgium. These rivers and their smaller branches form the delta with its many islands. Together with numerous canals, the rivers give important shipping access to the interior of Europe.

ABOVE: *The Maas River flows through the town of Maastricht in Limburg Province.*

European Hare

Fairly common on grassland and farmland, the European hare is easily distinguishable from the rabbit in that it has a larger, slimmer body, longer legs, and long, dark-tipped ears. In color, the hare's fur is also a warmer brown. During the early spring courtship period, the males chase and spar with each other. Grasses are their chief diet, although they will also eat root-crop leaves, vegetables, and tree bark. Unlike rabbits, hares do not burrow. Instead, they rest on the ground in a shallow scrape known as a form. Lying quietly like this, they can see danger approaching from all sides because of the placement of their eyes at the top of their heads. The young, or leverets, are born fully furred and active, with open eyes. They are suckled for a few weeks before leaving their mother to fend for themselves.

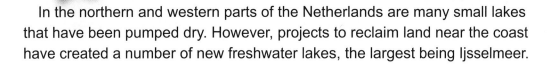

In the northern and western parts of the Netherlands are many small lakes that have been pumped dry. However, projects to reclaim land near the coast have created a number of new freshwater lakes, the largest being Ijsselmeer.

Trees, Plants & Wildlife

Over the centuries, human activity has permanently altered the natural landscape of the Netherlands in many ways. Because land is scarce and fully developed, areas of natural plant life are rare. A number of national parks and nature reserves have been established to protect the remaining areas of natural landscape.

ABOVE: *Veluwezoom National Park is located in the province of Gelderland. The park consists of forests and heather-covered heathland, which is kept open by grazing cattle. Animals that inhabit the area are red deer, wild boar, badger, and the regionally rare pine marten.*

The forests, the tall grasses of the dunes, and the heather of the heaths provide important habitats for roe deer, rabbits, hares, and small numbers of wild boar. The forests, mainly of oak, beech, ash, and pine, are carefully planned and protected by the government. Agricultural land (in particular, pasture for grazing animals) provides habitats for many species of migratory birds. Recent environmental projects have increased the number of wetlands, providing habitats for a number of species, including the newly reintroduced beaver and otter.

Text-Dependent Questions

1. How much of the Netherlands has been reclaimed from the sea?

2. How much of the Netherlands is below sea level?

3. What type of climate does the Netherlands have?

Research Project

Make a list of all the rivers, places, seas, and islands that you have read about in this chapter and mark them on a map of the Netherlands.

Words to Understand

cockade: An ornament (such as a rosette) usually worn on a hat as a badge.

euthanasia: The act or practice of killing someone who is very sick or injured in order to prevent any more suffering.

nationalist: A member of a political group advocating or fighting for national independence.

BELOW: Since the time when the Rhine Valley became incorporated into the Roman Empire, the river has been one of Europe's leading transport routes. The river, photographed here, flows through Wageningen, a historic town that dates back to the Middle Ages.

Chapter Two

THE GOVERNMENT & HISTORY OF THE NETHERLANDS

The Netherlands has not always existed as the unified country it is today. For centuries, the area was more of a cultural region than a nation. It was comprised of many territories, each fairly independent, and loosely united as a republic. The people of these territories had a common language, religion, and culture, but they were not united under one centralized government until the establishment of the modern monarchy in 1815.

The Netherlands in Ancient Times

The Netherlands has been inhabited since the last ice age; the oldest artifacts that have been found are 100,000 years old. During this time, the Netherlands was comprised largely of tundra with very scarce vegetation. The area's first inhabitants were hunter-gatherers, who lived during the last ice age. After the end of the ice age, various Paleolithic groups inhabited the area. Later, the first notable remains of Dutch prehistory were erected, the dolmens, which are large stone burial markers. Found in the province of Drenthe, they were probably built between 4100 and 3200 BCE. By the time the ancient Romans arrived in the region, the Netherlands was inhabited by various Germanic tribes, such as the Tubanti, the Canninefates, the Frisians, and the Batavii, who had settled there around 600 BCE. The Batavii were sometimes regarded as the "true" forefathers of the Dutch by later nationalist scholars.

In the first century CE, the Romans conquered the southern part of the Netherlands, where they built the first cities and created the Roman province of Germania Inferior. For most of the area of Roman occupation in the Netherlands, the boundary of the Roman Empire lay along the Rhine River. Romans built the first cities in the Netherlands. The most important of these

Educational Video

The Dutch monarchy explained.

ABOVE: *The central historic square in the ancient city center of Nijmegen. The city was originally a Roman settlement.*

were Utrecht, Nijmegen, and Maastricht. The Romans also introduced writing. Even the northern part of the Netherlands that lay outside Roman control was heavily influenced by the civilization that flourished to the south. Roman civilization in the area was eventually overrun by the mass migration of Germanic peoples, an event later known as the Völkerwanderung.

After the collapse of Roman authority, the Franks, a Germanic tribe, emerged as the dominant power in the region. Charlemagne, a Frank and the greatest ruler of the era, built an empire that extended over the territory of the Netherlands, Germany, France, and much of central Italy. Civil wars followed Charlemagne's death, and his sons divided their father's empire into three kingdoms.

The Holy Roman Empire

Eventually, the Frank dynasty died out in Germany and gave way to the Saxons. Otto I, a strong Saxon emperor, founded the Holy Roman Empire in 962 CE. The Holy Roman Empire was a group of western and central

Dating Systems and Their Meaning

You might be accustomed to seeing dates expressed with the abbreviations BC or AD, as in the year 1000 BC or the year AD 1900. For centuries, this dating system has been the most common in the Western world. However, since BC and AD are based on Christianity (BC stands for Before Christ and AD stands for anno Domini, Latin for "in the year of our Lord"), many people now prefer to use abbreviations that people from all religions can be comfortable using. The abbreviations BCE (meaning Before Common Era) and CE (meaning Common Era) mark time in the same way (for example, 1000 BC is the same year as 1000 BCE, and AD 1900 is the same year as 1900 CE), but BCE and CE do not have the same religious overtones as BC and AD.

ABOVE: *Charlemagne by Albrecht Dürer.*

ABOVE: *A replica of the Magdeburger Reiter, which depicts King Otto I.*

European territories that stood united by their faith in Roman Catholicism. While there was one supreme emperor, each territory had its own individual ruler. Constant struggles between these rulers and the empire marked the period. The crown and the Roman Catholic Church were also locked in a power struggle.

At its peak, the empire contained most of the territory that makes up the Netherlands today, as well as modern-day Germany, Austria, Slovenia, Switzerland, Belgium, Luxembourg, the Czech Republic, eastern France, northern Italy, and western Poland. Unfortunately, the Holy Roman Empire was not able to maintain political unity. The local nobility turned their tiny principalities and duchies into private kingdoms. There was little sense of obligation to the emperor, who governed over many parts of the nation in name only.

The various feudal states faced almost continual war, especially Utrecht and Holland. Through inheritance and conquest, the Netherlands eventually became a possession of the Habsburg dynasty under Charles V in the sixteenth century, who united the different principalities into one state. In 1548, Emperor Charles V granted the Netherlands status as an entity separate from both the Holy Roman Empire and from France. This act, the Pragmatic

Sanction of 1548, did not grant the Netherlands full independence, but it allowed significant autonomy.

The Reformation and the Eighty Years' War

The sixteenth century brought a new age to Europe: the Reformation. People began to question the practices of the Roman Catholic Church. This led to the creation of a new Christian group, the Protestants, or those who protest. In 1517, Martin Luther, a German monk, led a revolt against the Catholic Church, and Protestant teachings quickly gained a following throughout the region.

Charles V was succeeded by his son, Philip II of Spain. Unlike his father, who had been raised in Belgium, Philip had little interest in the Netherlands and the surrounding areas (otherwise known as the Low Countries), and thus was perceived as cold and detached by the local nobility. A devout Catholic, Philip was disgusted by the success of the Reformation in the Low Countries, which had led to the increasing popularity of Calvinism in the region. His attempts to enforce religious persecution of the Protestants and his efforts to centralize government, the justice system, and taxes made him unpopular and led to a revolt.

The Dutch fought for their independence from Spain, leading to the Eighty Years' War

ABOVE: *Emperor Charles V (1500–58) by Titian.*

ABOVE: *Martin Luther (1483–1546), portrait by Lucas Cranach the Elder.*

Is It Netherlands or Holland? And Where Does Dutch Come From?

Many English speakers consider Holland and Netherlands to be synonyms—different words for the same nation. Actually, however, Holland used to be a country, but it is no longer. Today, Holland is a region in the modern nation of the Netherlands; the old kingdom of Holland is now divided into two provinces, North Holland and South Holland.

The word "Dutch," meanwhile, is used to refer to the language and the people of the Netherlands. It is derived from *theodisk*, a word meaning "of the people." Some people from the Netherlands prefer the term Netherlandic, since the word *Dietsch* (the Dutch word for "Dutch") is so similar to *Deutsch* (the German word for "German").

(1568–1648). Seven rebellious provinces united in the Union of Utrecht in 1579 and formed the Republic of the Seven United Netherlands. William of Orange, the nobleman from whom every Dutch monarch is descended, led the Dutch during the first part of the war. The earliest years of the war were a success for the Spanish forces. They recaptured Antwerp and other important cities. However, subsequent sieges in Holland were countered by the Dutch, and later developments in the war favored the new republic. It recaptured most of the territory in the Netherlands. The Peace of Westphalia, signed January 30, 1648, confirmed the independence of the United Provinces from Spain.

The Golden Age

During the Eighty Years' War, the Dutch began to engage in overseas trade on a large scale. They hunted whales near Svalbard, and traded spices with India and Indonesia via the Dutch East India Company. The Dutch East India Company was the first company in history to issue shares of stock and was responsible for Dutch colonialism. During this period the Dutch founded colonies in Brazil, New Amsterdam (now New York), South Africa, and the West Indies. The Calvinist nation flourished culturally and economically as the dramatic increase in wealth and prosperity began to feed a resurgence in the arts and literature. Due to these developments, the seventeenth century is often called the Golden Age of the Netherlands.

The Netherlands was now a republic, largely governed by an aristocracy of city-merchants called the regents, rather than by a king. Every city and province had its own government and laws, and a large degree of autonomy. After attempts to find a competent sovereign proved unsuccessful, it was decided that sovereignty would be vested in the various provincial estates, the governing bodies of the provinces. The States General, a legislative body with representatives from all the provinces, would decide matters important to the republic as a whole. However, at the head of each province was a "stadtholder," a position held by a descendant of the House of Orange. Usually one stadtholder had authority over several provinces.

Following international recognition of the independence of the Netherlands, the republic began to experience a decline. In 1650, the stadtholder William II, Prince of Orange died leaving the nation without a powerful ruler. Since the conception of the republic, there had been an ongoing struggle for power between the regents and the House of Orange. Foreign enemies sought to take advantage of the lack of a strong centralized government in hope of gaining Dutch colonial holdings. A series of wars with England, France, and Spain drained the economy, and by the end of the eighteenth century, political unrest had come to a head.

ABOVE: *William II, Prince of Orange (1626–50) by Gerard van Honthorst.*

ABOVE: King William I (1772–1843) by Joseph Paelinck.

The Napoleonic Era and the Establishment of the Monarchy

As time went on, there was increasing conflict between the Orangists, who wanted stadtholder William V of Orange to hold more power, and the Patriots, who (under the influence of the American and French revolutions) wanted a more democratic form of government. In 1785, there was an armed rebellion by the Patriots.

The Orangist reaction was severe. No one dared appear in public without an orange **cockade** for fear of being lynched, and a small unpaid Prussian army was invited to occupy the Netherlands by the Orangists. The unpaid soldiers wasted little time before they began supporting themselves with looting and extortion.

When the French general Napoleon Bonaparte invaded and occupied the Netherlands in 1795, his troops encountered very little united resistance. William V of Orange fled to England in advance of the French army. The French occupation of the Netherlands ended in 1813 after Napoleon was defeated, a defeat in which William

V played a prominent role. After the Napoleonic occupation, the Netherlands was put back on the map of Europe. In 1815, the country became a monarchy, with William V, the Prince of Orange, crowned King William I. By 1848, political unrest across Europe convinced King William II to agree to liberal and democratic reforms, rewriting the constitution, and transforming the Netherlands into a constitutional monarchy. The new document was proclaimed valid on November 3 of that year. As the nineteenth century came to a close, the nation prospered, expanding its colonial holdings in the Pacific and extending to its citizens freedoms and civil liberties that were very liberal for the age.

The Netherlands and the World Wars

World War I began on June 28, 1914, when Gavrilo Princip, a Serbian nationalist, assassinated Austrian archduke Ferdinand and his wife, Sophie. Russia allied with Serbia. Germany sided with Austria and soon declared war on Russia. After France declared its support for Russia, Germany attacked France. German troops then invaded Belgium, a neutral country, as it stood between German forces and Paris. Great Britain declared war on Germany.

Although the Netherlands remained neutral in the conflict, it did not escape unharmed because the whole country was literally surrounded by nations at war. The German invasion of Belgium led to an influx of nearly one million refugees from that country. The North Sea became unsafe for civilian ships to sail, and food became scarce. An error in food distribution caused the aptly named Potato Rebellion in Amsterdam in 1917, when rioters robbed a food transport intended for soldiers.

The Netherlands found itself economically crippled following the war, and the nation's fortunes did not improve greatly as it struggled with the challenges caused by the Great Depression. The Depression led to mass unemployment and poverty, as well as increasing social instability. Riots broke out in Amsterdam, requiring the intervention of the army. Concern was also mounting over the rise of Adolph Hitler in neighboring Germany.

At the outbreak of World War II in 1939, the Netherlands declared its neutrality again. However, on May 10, 1940, Germany launched an attack on the Netherlands and Belgium, quickly overrunning most of the country and fighting against a poorly equipped Dutch army. The nation's rapid defeat, though, affected only the Royal Netherlands Army. The Royal Netherlands Navy, the Royal Air Force, and the Netherlands East Indies Army, stationed in the Dutch East Indies, were still left operational, so the Netherlands did not cease to fight. This proved to be vitally important to the governing of the overseas territories and the continuing resistance against Germany.

The royal family and some military forces managed to escape to Britain before Japanese troops invaded the Dutch East Indies on January 11, 1942. The Dutch, weakened by the Nazi occupation at home, surrendered on March 8, after Japanese troops landed on the island of Java. Dutch citizens

ABOVE: *In 1934, Hitler became Germany's head of state, with the title of* Führer und Reichskanzler *(Leader and Chancellor of the Reich).*

were captured and put to work in forced labor camps. However, many Dutch ships and military personnel managed to escape to Australia, from where they were able to continue to fight against the Japanese.

Shortly after the invasion the persecution of Jews began. The Germans established a "Jewish Board" as a way of organizing the identification and deportation of Jews more efficiently. When the Germans had gathered enough information, they started deporting the Jews to concentration camps. The Dutch people protested the deportations with a strike, which accomplished little except to encourage the Germans to impose harsher restrictions on the occupied Dutch. The consequences for the Jewish community were catastrophic; less than one-quarter of all Dutch Jews survived the war. Perhaps the nation's best recognized victim of the Holocaust is Anne Frank, a young girl who became famous years later because of her diary, written while she was in hiding from the Nazis. The Franks were eventually found, and Anne died in a concentration camp.

The occupied Dutch suffered greatly under Nazi control. *Arbeitseinsatz* was imposed on the Netherlands, which obliged every man between the ages of eighteen and forty-five to work in the German factories, which were bombed every night by the Allies. Food and many other goods were taken out of the Netherlands to supply German troops. Over time, rationing became a way of controlling the people; any Dutch people who violated German laws automatically lost their food. Hiding Jews was even more dangerous, as it was punishable by death; as a result, one-third of the Dutch people who hid Jews did not survive the war.

ABOVE: *A photograph of Anne Frank in 1940.*

These harsh measures helped feed the growth of the Dutch resistance movement, where many brave Dutch people operated in secret against the Nazis. Resistance activities included the hiding of Jews and other endangered people, such as Allied soldiers and airmen who were stranded behind enemy lines; the collection of intelligence about Nazi troop movements and supply lines; and the publication of newspapers with news from abroad.

Following the Allied invasion of Normandy on D-Day, Allied forces moved quickly to liberate the Netherlands. A joint American and British operation, code-named "Operation Market Garden," was executed in hope of liberating the Dutch. Unfortunately, losses were heavy, and the Allies were unable to cross the Rhine River. The end result was that the region south of the river was liberated by September of 1944, while the rest of the country had to wait until the German surrender in May 1945. That winter is known as the "hunger winter" because of the large number of Dutch people who starved.

The Netherlands Today

The postwar years marked a period of tremendous change and growth for the Netherlands. Two days after the surrender of Japan, most of the Dutch East Indies declared its independence as Indonesia. Although it was initially thought that the loss of the territory would lead to an economic downfall, the reverse proved to be true, and in the decades that followed, the Dutch economy experienced unprecedented growth.

The Government of the Netherlands

The Netherlands has been a constitutional monarchy since 1815. The head of state is the monarch, presently King Willem-Alexander van Oranje Nassau, but the sovereign's power is mostly for ceremonial and representative functions. The chief of the government is the prime minister, who is appointed by the king. The constitution lays down that the monarch and the ministers together constitute the government. It also lists the basic civil and social rights of the Dutch citizens. The ministers and state secretaries are responsible for the day-to-day business of government. The Netherlands has a multiparty system, usually governed by a coalition of different political parties. Every four years, a new government is chosen.

ABOVE: *Located in the center of the Hague on the Hofvijver (Royal Pond), the Binnenhof is a complex of buildings that house the Dutch parliament. The location has been the center of Dutch government since the fifteenth century. The Binnenhof is open to the public and so visitors can join a daily tour of the complex.*

The rapid economic growth of the postwar period was critical to the development of the Dutch society of today. The small country soon had difficulty meeting the increased labor needs of its robust economy and began encouraging immigration as a way to meet them.

The postwar years were also a time of great social and cultural changes. Although the nation has been largely homogeneous for most of its history, today the Netherlands is a truly multicultural society as a result of immigration from countries such as Turkey and Morocco, as well as from former colonies in Asia, Africa, and the Caribbean. In the face of the challenges posed by life in the twentieth century, the changes in Dutch culture that evolved from mass immigration, and the expansion of popular culture, traditional sources of authority began to be of less importance. Young people, students in particular, rejected traditional morals, and pushed for change in matters like women's rights, sexuality, and environmental issues. Today, the Netherlands is regarded as a very liberal country, with pragmatic policies on matters such as drug use, prostitution, and legalized euthanasia. Same-sex marriage became legal in 2001.

Following the struggles of World War II, the Netherlands decided to pursue a more prominent place in world affairs. Shortly after the war's end, the country

ABOVE: *King Willem-Alexander of the Netherlands waves to the crowd following the royal couple's regional visit to the province of Flevoland in 2017.*

sought a series of political and economic alliances. The Benelux Economic Union was signed in 1944 between Belgium, the Netherlands, and Luxembourg, and it came into effect in 1948 to promote the free movement of workers, capital, services, and goods in the region. It was the earliest precursor to the European Union (EU), though other organizations that led to the development of the EU were founded later (the ECSC in 1951 and the EEC in 1957). The three Benelux countries were also founding members of these intermediate organizations, together with West Germany, France, and Italy.

A modern, industrialized nation, the Netherlands is also an active member of the United Nations. The country was a founding member of NATO and adopted the euro in 2001. In recent years, the Dutch have often been a driving force behind the integration of more Central and Eastern European countries in the EU.

Text-Dependent Questions

1. Name two Dutch cities that were originally Roman settlements.

2. When did Germany attack the Netherlands during WWII?

3. What was "Operation Market Garden?"

Research Project

Write a brief report on Dutch colonialism.

The Formation of the European Union (EU)

The EU is a confederation of European nations that continues to grow. As of 2017, there are twenty-eight official members. Several other candidates are also waiting for approval. All countries that enter the EU agree to follow common laws about foreign security policies. They also agree to cooperate on legal matters that go on within the EU. The European Council meets to discuss all international matters and make decisions about them. Each country's own concerns and interests are important, though. And apart from legal and financial issues, the EU tries to uphold values such as peace, human dignity, freedom, and equality.

All member countries remain autonomous. This means that they generally keep their own laws and regulations. The idea for a union among European nations was first mentioned after World War II. The war had devastated much of Europe, both physically and financially. In 1950, the French foreign minister suggested that France and West Germany combine their coal and steel industries under one authority. Both countries would have control over the

ABOVE: *The entrance to the European Union Parliament Building in Brussels.*

Member Countries

Austria	Greece	Romania
Belgium	Hungary	Slovakia
Bulgaria	Ireland	Slovenia
Croatia	Italy	Spain
Cyprus	Latvia	Sweden
Czech Republic	Lithuania	United Kingdom
Denmark	Luxembourg	*(Brexit: For the time*
Estonia	Malta	*being, the United*
Finland	Netherlands	*Kingdom remains a full*
France	Poland	*member of the EU.)*
Germany	Portugal	

industries. This would help them become more financially stable. It would also make war between the countries much more difficult. The idea was interesting to other European countries as well. In 1951, France, West Germany, Belgium, Luxembourg, the Netherlands, and Italy signed the Treaty of Paris, creating the European Coal and Steel Community. These six countries would become the core of the EU.

In 1957, these same countries signed the Treaties of Rome, creating the European Economic Community. In 1965, the Merger Treaty formed the European Community. Finally, in 1992, the Maastricht Treaty was signed. This treaty defined the European Union. It gave a framework for expanding the EU's political role, particularly in the area of foreign and security policy. It would also replace national currencies with the euro. The next year, the treaty went into effect. At that time, the member countries included the original six plus another six who had joined during the 1970s and '80s.

In the following years, the EU would take more steps to form a single market for its members. This would make joining the union even more advantageous. In addition to enlargement, the EU is steadily becoming more integrated through its own policies for closer cooperation between member states.

Words to Understand

automated: An automatic manufactured process.

biomass: Organic matter that can be converted to fuel.

entrepreneurial: A person who can be described as having good initiative, business skills, and is prepared to take risks to succeed.

BELOW: Greenhouse horticulture is a vital part of the Netherlands' economy. The plant-growing environment can be controlled throughout the year. Temperature, levels of light and shade, irrigation, fertilizer application, and atmospheric humidity can all be finely tuned to ensure maximum yield.

Chapter Three
THE DUTCH ECONOMY

In 2008, the entire world entered an economic recession, and the Netherlands did not escape this global financial crisis. A protracted recession followed until 2013, during which time unemployment doubled and household spending contracted. Since then, however, austerity measures have improved public finances. In 2016, the government budget returned to a surplus and economic growth finally surpassed prerecession levels. The Dutch government projects steady but modest economic growth going forward and expects unemployment to decrease further.

ABOVE: *A Dutch fishing boat in the North Sea. The Netherlands has a long maritime history and fishing has always been important to its economy.*

A Social Market Economy

The long-term success of the Dutch economy is largely due to its structure as a social market economy. A social market economy has both material (financial) and social (human) dimensions.

The two main components of a market economy are **entrepreneurial** responsibility and competition. It is an entrepreneur's responsibility to see to her company's growth and to ensure that it can adapt to changing circumstances. Competition ensures that new products and technologies will constantly be developed as each business works to ensure that their product best meets the needs of the consumer. The government's role is limited to creating conditions

ABOVE: *Delft Blue pottery has been in production in Delft since the seventeenth century and is world famous. Today, there is only one factory left still producing the blue pottery by traditional methods. Miniature Delft houses, such as these ones, can be bought from any of Delft's souvenir shops.*

Cheese Production in the Netherlands

The Dutch produce 1,433 million pounds (650 million kg) of cheese every year. A third of this is for domestic consumption, the other two-thirds are exported, making the Netherlands the largest cheese exporter in the world. The Dutch are big cheese-eaters, consuming on average 31 pounds (14.3 kg) of cheese per person per year. The most popular cheeses are Gouda and Edam. However, there are many other types, including Frisian, Limburger, Maasland, Texelaar-Kollumer, Leyden, and Leerdammer.

favorable to a healthy economy by contributing to the infrastructure, as well as fair labor and tax laws. The government also provides assistance to those unable to cope with the greater demands of a competitive market.

The New Economy

As is happening in many industrialized nations, a shift has been made away from manufacturing as the primary source of economic growth. Although around one-quarter of the Netherlands' gross domestic product (GDP) still comes from its manufacturing enterprises, the dominant source of the Netherland's income today comes from the service sector, which contributes 70.2 percent of the country's GDP. The largest service industry is trade, followed by transportation and telecommunications, construction, banking and insurance, and other financial services. The three largest banks are ABN Amro, Rabobank, and ING, which operate worldwide, serving Dutch and foreign businesses and governments.

The Netherlands is an important center for multinational businesses. Its benefits include an advanced infrastructure for telecommunications and goods and passenger transport. In addition, many foreign companies come to the

Netherlands because of its central geographic location, its flexible working hours, and its educated, multilingual workforce. The port of Rotterdam and Schiphol airport are the two most important international transportation hubs. Many Dutch companies have subsidiaries in other countries.

Industry: The Mainstay of the Economy and Exports

Heavy industry is still an important part of the Dutch economy. More than a third of the country's GDP is dependent on the export of manufactured goods. The Dutch manufacturing sector has a broad international outlook. Dutch manufacturers export all over the world, have branches in many countries, and often form alliances with foreign companies. The primary manufacturing industries are chemicals, food processing, and metalworking. There are also

ABOVE: Heineken is a famous Dutch brand and exporter of pale lager beer. Most of it is produced at its facility in Zoeterwoude in the Netherlands.

ABOVE: *An aerial view of the state-of-the-art terminal for storage of mineral oil products and chemicals at Rotterdam Botlek.*

highly developed printing and electrical engineering enterprises. Production processes in all these industries have been largely **automated** in the past ten years, making them strongly competitive on world markets, with plants both in the Netherlands and abroad.

The Netherlands is home to the world's largest chemical companies. The Dutch metalworking industry specializes in building machinery. The advanced electronic control systems make the Dutch world leaders in the manufacture of vehicles, food-processing equipment, and machinery for the chemical industry. This has also promoted the growth of a thriving electronics industry. The main markets for Dutch-manufactured goods are Germany, France, Belgium, and Britain. The Netherlands is the second-largest supplier of industrial equipment and consumer goods to these very demanding markets. Germany imports more from the Netherlands than from either the United States or Britain.

Agriculture

Agricultural practices in the Netherlands are among the most sophisticated and environmentally sound in the world. High labor costs are constantly pushing the agriculture sector in the Netherlands to further automate production processes. For several decades, environmental legislation has also been forcing the sector to come up with cleaner and smarter products and systems.

Today's Dutch farmer is a manager. He runs his business using the data generated for him every day by sophisticated computer systems. His cows are milked by robots, which keep precise records of their production. One look at a computer screen makes it easy to see that the temperature of the milk produced by one of his cows is not quite right, or that they are not producing

ABOVE: *The Netherlands is world famous for its flower bulbs that are produced for export. The country also has many farms producing just cut flowers.*

The Economy of the Netherlands

Gross Domestic Product (GDP): $872.8 billion (2016 est.)
GDP Per Capita: $51,200 (2016 est.)
Industries: agroindustries, metal and engineering products, electrical machinery and equipment, chemicals, petroleum, construction, microelectronics, fishing
Agriculture: vegetables, ornamentals, dairy, poultry and livestock products, propagation materials
Export Commodities: machinery and transport equipment, chemicals, mineral fuels, food and livestock, manufactured goods
Export Partners: Germany 24.1%, Belgium 10.7%, UK 9.4%, France 8.8%, Italy 4.2% (2016)
Import Commodities: machinery and transport equipment, chemicals, fuels, foodstuffs, clothing
Import Partners: Germany 15.3%, China 14.1%, Belgium 8.4%, US 7.9%, UK 5.3%, Russia 4.1% (2016)
Currency: euro

Source: www.cia.gov 2017

enough milk. The farmer then has a series of diagnostic programs to help him identify and correct the problem. Agricultural technology has changed the face of farming forever.

As a small country, the Netherlands faces specific problems, particularly in relation to environmental protection. One problem that the Dutch have addressed successfully is the reduction of ammonia gases emitted by manure. Ammonia produced by manure is a major source of air pollution. The manure therefore has to be worked into the soil with purpose-built vehicles. In the field of animal housing technology, special grid floors and air-conditioning systems have been developed to prevent excessive concentrations of ammonia entering the environment. The Dutch have been so successful in developing agricultural technology that these systems have become important as technology and goods for export. For example, three of the four milking systems used worldwide were developed in the Netherlands.

Energy

Giant natural gas reserves lie in the northern area of the Netherlands, making it Western Europe's second-largest producer. Drilling companies operate gas and oil fields both on land and in the North Sea. The port of Rotterdam is a crucial link in Western Europe's energy supply chain. Large quantities of crude oil arrive there by ship for distribution throughout the region. The port has many

ABOVE: *North Sea oil and gas is a major economic component of the Dutch economy. This rig is situated off the coast near Harlingen.*

Educational Video

The Netherlands is the second-largest exporter of agricultural products in the world. Not bad for a small country.

refineries and terminals, and pipelines transport crude oil and oil-based products directly to the industrial centers of Germany and Belgium.

The presence of refineries and offshore installations has led to a wide range of activities serving the oil and gas industries. Four large steel construction firms, for instance, design and build entire refineries and offshore installations. Dozens of other Dutch companies produce other related equipment. Several Dutch research institutions have laboratories that simulate offshore conditions.

In recent years, the Netherlands' government has introduced strict environmental legislation. This has encouraged researchers to develop technologies for purifying wastewater, neutralizing waste gases, and processing industrial and domestic pollutants. Dutch manufacturing plants are now among the world's cleanest. Around forty Dutch companies are currently making electricity generators driven by alternative energy sources such as **biomass**, sunlight, or wind. In 2016, 12.2 percent of the nation's electricity came from these renewable sources. The EU has set a target for 20 percent of production from renewables by 2020, so the Netherlands has a fair way to go.

Transportation

The Netherlands is the hub of a complex transportation network comprising air, sea, river, highway, and rail links extending in all directions. Rotterdam is the world's largest port, and millions of tons of cargo are loaded and unloaded there every day. Schiphol International Airport is the fifth-busiest passenger airport in Europe. The Netherlands accounts for 53 percent of all the river transport on the Rhine and the Maas, and nearly a third of all European trucks make use of Dutch highways.

Working for a Brighter Future

The Netherlands is a country with relatively few natural resources. As a result, it has had to create wealth primarily by developing and applying knowledge. Such collaboration is known as the "Polder Model" and refers to the way the Dutch have applied their knowledge and worked together to reclaim land from the sea. The same dedication can be seen in the way the Dutch approach research and the development of new technology.

ABOVE: *Schiphol Airport, Amsterdam, is the most important airport in the Netherlands and one of the busiest international airports in Europe.*

More than 60,000 researchers work in Dutch companies, universities, and research institutes. These researchers produce 7 percent of the EU's scientific publications and hold 6 percent of its patents. Several development projects for knowledge infrastructure are currently in progress, with more than 200 million euros in funding allocated for this work. These projects are forging connections between companies, educational institutions, and government in areas such as miniaturization, hydraulic engineering in delta areas, traffic and transport, biotechnology, and data communications.

As the Dutch look toward the future, they are hopeful that this continued investment into research and new technology will help create not only a stronger economy and more prosperous country, but a cleaner and safer world.

Text-Dependent Questions

1. When did the Netherlands recover from the global financial crisis of 2008?

2. What percentage of the Netherlands' GDP comes from the service sector?

3. What is the "Polder Model?"

Research Project

Write a brief report on Dutch agriculture and industry.

Words to Understand

culture: The habits, beliefs, and traditions of a particular people, place, or time.

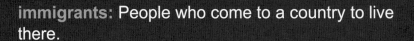

immigrants: People who come to a country to live there.

minority: A part of a population that is in some ways (as in race or religion) different from others.

BELOW: The Oosterscheldekering barrier connects the Zeeland islands of Schouwen-Duiveland and Noord-Beveland. It was built to protect the Zeeland region from flooding. The barrier is a fine example of Dutch hydraulic engineering and definitely worth a visit.

Chapter Four
CITIZENS OF THE NETHERLANDS: PEOPLE, CUSTOMS & CULTURE

The Netherlands, home to over 17 million people, is one of the world's most densely populated countries. The tiny country has more than 1,000 inhabitants per square mile (more than 400 inhabitants per square kilometer). There are two official languages, Dutch and Frisian, both Germanic languages. Frisian is only spoken in the northern province of Friesland; it is the language that most closely resembles English. According to local tradition, it is said that farmers from the north of England can converse with their Frisian counterparts about their shared livelihoods without difficulty.

ABOVE: The Dutch are a nation of cyclists. The flat terrain means that getting around on a bicycle is relatively easy.

ABOVE: *West-Terschelling is a village on Terschelling island, on the Wadden Sea, in the province of Friesland. The languages spoken here are Dutch and Frisian. Interestingly, Frisian is a language very closely related to English.*

Ethnic minorities make up around 20 percent of the Netherlands' population. **Immigrants**, mostly from Turkey, Morocco, and Italy, account for most of these minority groups. Many of these immigrants have adapted to Dutch language and **culture**, assisted by the ability of **minority** communities to obtain government funding to set up their own schools. It is possible, therefore, for a Moroccan child living in the Netherlands to attend a publicly funded school where her lessons are taught in both Dutch and Arabic.

ABOVE: *A vegetable market in Bijlmer, southeast Amsterdam. Despite having some problems in the past, Bijlmer is now home to a vibrant multicultural community.*

Religion

The Dutch people have full freedom to choose their faith and religion. The Netherlands is now one of the most secular countries in Europe; an estimated 42 percent of the population is nonreligious. The remainder are 30 percent Roman Catholic, around 20 percent Protestant, and over 5 percent Muslim. Protestants used to be the largest religious group in the Netherlands, but, over the past century, the older Protestant churches have seen a rapid decline. Islam has begun to gain a foothold in recent years, mostly to the large number of immigrants from the Middle East.

ABOVE: *The Basilica of Saint Nicholas is centrally located in the old part of Amsterdam. This beautiful Catholic church was designed by Adrianus Bleijs, who used revival styles such as neo-baroque and neo-Renaissance.*

ABOVE: *Completed in 2015 and opened in 2016, Westermoskee or Ayasofya Mosque in Amsterdam, was designed by French architects Marc and Nada Breitman.*

Education

It is compulsory for children in the Netherlands to attend school full time from the age of five, and many attend school part time between the ages of sixteen and eighteen. The content taught in all types of schools is established by law, as are goals for proficiency. This enables the government to ensure that education standards are uniform throughout the country.

Schools set up by local governments are called public-authority schools. All other schools, founded by private bodies, are called private schools. Though more than three-quarters of the schools in the Netherlands are private, they are

Educational Video

The school system in the Netherlands.

all eligible for government funding, provided they meet some basic criteria. Teachers are also paid by the government. In 2001, the Netherlands spent more than 5 percent of its GDP on education. Education is free of charge for children up to the age of sixteen.

Primary schools in the Netherlands cater to children from ages four to twelve. The eight-year primary school curriculum focuses on pupils' emotional, intellectual, and artistic development, along with the acquisition of essential social, cultural, and physical skills. At the age of twelve, children are separated into one of three different kinds of schools: prevocational secondary school, which takes four years to complete; general secondary school, which takes five years to complete; or pre-university school, which takes six years to complete. Parents of students between the ages of sixteen and eighteen are required to pay for textbooks and other teaching materials. This is offset by the child benefit that all Dutch parents receive from the government for children under the age of eighteen.

Students eighteen or older have to pay for their education. Fees for most university courses are the same. All students over eighteen receive a basic government grant, which they may supplement with a loan. The amount of the loan will depend on the student's income. The student's academic achievement also plays a role. The Dutch government invests heavily in education, and, as a result, the Dutch people are highly literate, and many are fluent in more than one language.

ABOVE: *Leiden University, Leiden, was founded in 1575 by William, Prince of Orange, and is the oldest university in the Netherlands. It has seven faculties, fifty departments, and houses numerous national and international research institutes.*

Food and Drink

In the Netherlands it is common to have two cold meals and one hot meal a day. Bread, fruit, and cheese are generally eaten with breakfast and lunch. Sometimes crisp bread, crackers, rye bread, or cereal flakes called muesli are substituted for the bread. Dinner usually begins with soup, and the main course consists of boiled potatoes, vegetables, and roasted meat or fish. Rice, other grains, or pasta sometimes take the place of the potatoes. Dessert is usually yogurt, cold custard, or fruit.

The Netherlands is famous for its dairy products, especially its cheeses. Traditional Dutch cheeses include Gouda, Edam, and Leyden.

ABOVE: The medieval market square in Gouda is where the famous cheese market is also held. For more than 300 years, cheese has been traded here.

Oliebollen
(Traditional Dutch Doughnuts)

Makes 4 to 6 servings

Ingredients
2 cups milk
1 tablespoon of sugar
½ teaspoon of salt
2 tablespoons butter
¼ cup warm water
1 small package cake yeast
3 cups flour
1 egg
½ cup raisins

Directions
Scald milk, stir in sugar, salt, and butter. Let cool. Pour warm water into a bowl and sprinkle in yeast. Stir until dissolved. Add milk mixture, egg, ½ cup of flour, and raisins. Beat until smooth. Stir in remaining flour. Cover and let rise for 1 hour or until it doubles in size. Beat batter down and deep-fry spoonfuls of dough until brown. Sprinkle with powdered sugar when done.

Appelkoek
(Dutch Apple Cake)

Makes 6 servings

Ingredients
2–3 medium apples
1½ cups flour
3½ teaspoons baking powder
6 tablespoons granulated sugar, divided
¼ cup margarine or butter
¾ cup milk
1 egg, well beaten
½ teaspoon ground cinnamon

Directions
Peel and cut the apples into eighths (wedges). Sift together flour, baking powder with 4 tablespoons of the sugar. Cut the butter/margarine. Combine egg and milk and add to flour mixture. Turn batter into a greased 8-inch square cake pan. Press apple wedges partly into the batter. Combine the remaining 2 tablespoons of sugar and the cinnamon, sprinkle over the apples. Bake at 425°F for 25 to 30 minutes.

Arts and Architecture

The height of Dutch architecture was during the seventeenth century. Due to the thriving economy, Dutch cities expanded greatly during this period. New town halls, weighing houses, and storehouses were built. Merchants with newly obtained fortunes ordered houses built along one of the many new canals that were dug out in and around many cities. Many of these homes with their grand façades can still be seen and appreciated.

ABOVE: Rembrandt van Rijn.

ABOVE: Vincent van Gogh.

ABOVE: Maurits Cornelis Escher.

ABOVE: Piet Mondrian.

ABOVE: Girl with a Pearl Earring *(1665) by Johannes Vermeer.*

The Netherlands has produced many great artists over the centuries. From the paintings of Rembrandt van Rijn and Johannes Vermeer in the seventeenth century, to the genius of Vincent van Gogh in the nineteenth century, to the more modern works of Piet Mondrian and M. C. Escher, the Dutch have a proud artistic tradition.

ABOVE: *These ancient houses in Amsterdam almost look as if they are holding each other up. Their design is typical of Dutch architecture.*

ABOVE: *A homage to Dutch architecture—the Inntel Hotel in Zaandam.*

ABOVE: *Sinterklaas is a legendary figure based on Saint Nicholas. The feast of Sinterklaas is celebrated in the Netherlands on December 5 and 6 by people of all ages and beliefs.*

Festivals and Events

The Dutch really know how to celebrate a holiday. Parades, costume parties, crowded streets, floats, shows, and dances—the Dutch love a good party.

While the country only observes eight public holidays nationwide, many festivals and events are celebrated at a regional or national scale. These celebrations may be religious or secular in nature. One Dutch tradition that should be familiar to American children is Sinterklaas, celebrated on December 5 and 6.

There are some distinctions between Sinterklaas and Santa Claus, however. Santa lives at the North Pole, whereas Dutch children know that Sinterklaas is making his list of naughty and nice children on the sunny coast of Spain. Santa

ABOVE: Two great Dutch specialities, growing flowers and canal-faring, come together in a three-day-long floating procession across the region of Westland. The boats sail through Westland, Midden-Delfland, Vlaardingen, Rijswijk, the Hague, and Delft.

ABOVE: *The King's Day festivities take place on King Willem-Alexander's birthday in April. Festivities are held in the streets, on the canals, and in the parks. People traditionally dress up as the King or wear the King's insignia. Almost everyone taking part wears orange, the traditional color of the Netherlands.*

has an army of elves for helpers, whereas Sinterklaas has large, black-faced helpers called the *Zwarte Pieten*. Sinterklaas, as the legend goes, arrives in the Netherlands by steamer from his home in Spain a couple of weeks before his birthday. His arrival occurs at a designated port city each year, and the parade that follows is broadcast on national television. Actors dressed as the Saint and his black helpers enter town in large, colorful processions. The Saint rides a white horse, and his helpers poke fun at bystanders while throwing small ginger biscuits at them. Sinterklaas sightings are then common over the next several days. Finally, on December 5, children put their shoes by the fireplace in hopes that Sinterklaas will fill them with treats, assuming they have been good over the previous year. Bad children can expect to be deported to Spain by the Zwarte Pieten in the middle of the night.

Some controversy has developed in recent years over the blackface worn by actors impersonating the Zwarte Pieten. Some say this tradition reflects the soot the helpers picked up from the chimneys they went down. Others think they represent the feared Moors of old Spain, who were considered evil enough to frighten any medieval Dutch child into behaving. Some people today feel the blacking-up should stop as it represents an unacceptable racial stereotype. The picture of mischievous, black servants carrying out the wishes of a good, white master is distasteful to some observers, although most Dutch people still feel it is a harmless tradition. Nonetheless, whether the black makeup stays or goes, the feast of Sinterklaas is a shining example of the enthusiasm with which the Dutch celebrate their holidays.

Text-Dependent Questions

1. Which language is similar to Frisian?

2. What percentage of ethnic minorities make up the Netherlands' population?

3. What percentage of the people in the Netherlands have no religion at all?

Research Project

Select a favorite Dutch artist and create a work of art in the same style.

Words to Understand

mausoleum: A large stone building with places for entombment of the dead above ground.

medieval: Relating to the Middle Ages.

urban: Relating to or characteristic of a city.

BELOW: Traditional Dutch houses on the Oudezijds Voorburgwal Canal in central Amsterdam.

Chapter Five
THE FAMOUS CITIES OF THE NETHERLANDS

The Netherlands is an extremely **urban** society. More than 80 percent of its population lives in cities and towns. Most Dutch citizens earn a fairly comfortable income and lead prosperous lifestyles. Because land is at a premium, Dutch cities tend to be densely populated industrial centers, as most open land is reserved for agriculture. Nonetheless, the high population density and level of industrialization cannot diminish the appeal of these ancient cities, which brim with important architecture, cultural attractions, and significant historical sites.

Amsterdam: The Capital

Amsterdam is the capital of the Netherlands. Founded in the late twelfth century as a small fishing village on the banks of the Amstel River, it is now the nation's largest city and its financial and cultural center. As of 2016, the population of the greater Amsterdam area was approximately 1.6 million. The old city was built up around a series of concentric, semicircular canals, which still define the city's layout and appearance. Many fine examples

ABOVE: *Tourists wait in line at the Anne Frank House and Museum.*

Educational Video

A tourist's guide to Amsterdam.

ABOVE: *The Rijksmuseum is the national museum of the Netherlands, dedicated to Dutch arts and culture. The museum is located in Museum Square, Amsterdam, close to the Van Gogh Museum and the Stedelijk Museum.*

ABOVE: *Situated on the west side of Dam Square in the center of Amsterdam, the Royal Palace is one of three palaces used by the king.*

of Dutch architecture can be found among the houses and mansions situated along these canals; most are lived in, others are now offices, and some are public buildings.

Today, the city is noted for many outstanding museums, including the Rijksmuseum, the Van Gogh Museum, the Stedelijk Museum, Rembrandt House Museum, the Anne Frank House, and for its world-class symphony orchestra. It also has a quite different reputation for its red-light district, de Wallen, and the many coffee shops where marijuana is legally sold.

Delft Pottery

Delft is home to the world-famous Delft Blue pottery made in and around Delft in the Netherlands. The distinctive blue and white pottery has been in production since the seventeenth century. Delft Blue was originally created as an alternative to the more expensive porcelain originating in China. Unlike Chinese porcelain, the tin-glazed pottery made in Delft was not made from Chinese clay but composite clays. Centuries ago, there were dozens of active pottery factories; however, over time, nearly all of them have closed. Nowadays, Delftware is mainly bought by international tourists for souvenirs, although it is once again becoming popular with Dutch consumers, who are showing renewed interest in it.

Delft

Delft was granted a city charter in 1246, and original **medieval** structures of that period are still recognizable in the old city center. The town developed into a vibrant commercial town thanks to its textile industries, breweries, and shipping trade. In 1536, a major fire almost destroyed the town. Shortly afterward, it became the residence of the princes of Orange, Holland's royal family. William of Orange was living in Delft when he was murdered, and the bullet holes from the attack are still visible in the present Municipal

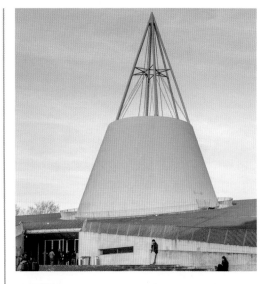

ABOVE: *Library, Delft University of Technology (also known as TU Delft).*

Museum. The prince's marble **mausoleum** can be admired in the New Church, over the vault of the royal family. The collection of the Military Museum in the old armory shows the military history of the House of Orange.

Delft is renowned all over the world as the birthplace of Delft pottery. In the seventeenth century, dozens of small pottery factories arose in Delft in buildings that formerly housed breweries. Delft was one of the home ports of the Dutch East India Company, and when the Delft potters became acquainted with imported Chinese porcelain, they began manufacturing Delftware with designs based on these patterns. It is still made by hand today.

ABOVE: *An aerial view of the beautiful city of Delft with the town hall in the foreground. Delft is the birthplace of the famous Dutch painter Johannes Vermeer.*

ABOVE: *Maastricht is the oldest city in the Netherlands and the capital city of the province of Limburg. It is where the Maastricht Treaty was signed on February 7, 1992, by the members of the European Community.*

Maastricht

The southernmost and sunniest city in the Netherlands, Maastricht, is a beautiful walled city of Roman origin set on the river Maas. The green, unspoiled hillsides that surround Maastricht are home to famous vineyards and provided the opportunity for many kinds of outdoor recreation. Architecture and history enthusiasts will not be disappointed either, since Maastricht has an abundance of ramparts, caves, tunnels, grottos, museums, and basilicas to explore.

The Hague

The history of the Hague begins in the thirteenth century, when the site was chosen as the ideal place for a hunting lodge by the counts of Holland. The elaborate hunting lodge drew other nobles who built their own grand houses, and a village for traders and craftsmen soon developed. In 1248, William II, Count of Holland, began the construction of a castle on the Binnenhof. William's son, Floris V, added the massive Knights' Hall, expanding a complex that today is the seat of the country's administrative government.

ABOVE: *Mauritshuis in the Hague is an art gallery that contains many great works by old masters such as Vermeer and Rembrandt.*

Today, the Hague is not only the official seat of government, it is also the home of the Dutch royal family. If the flag is raised at Huis Ten Bosch Palace, it means a member of the royal family is in residence. The royal family also has offices in Noordeinde Palace, in the city center. Each year, on the third Tuesday of September, the royal family rides in a golden coach to the Binnenhof. King Willem-Alexander also opens the new parliamentary year by making his annual address from the throne at the Ridderzaal.

Over the centuries, The Hague has grown into a cosmopolitan city; it now boast no fewer than three royal palaces, more than sixty foreign embassies, and the headquarters of innumerable international engineering, oil, and chemical concerns. The lush greenery of the original hunting grounds can still be seen in the large parks, gardens, and woods that continue to thrive within the city limits.

ABOVE: *Scheveningen is one of eight districts of the Hague. It is situated on the North Sea and has an extensive beach front.*

The Hague is perhaps best known as the International City of Peace and Justice. The International Criminal Court, the Peace Palace, the War Crimes Tribunal, and Europol are all headquartered here.

Rotterdam

Rotterdam derives its name from the Rotte River. In the thirteenth century, a fishing village was built near a dam in the Rotte. The village was granted a municipal charter in 1340 and grew into a prosperous trading town during the sixteenth and seventeenth centuries, with many warehouses and shipyards. By the late nineteenth century, Rotterdam had developed into an international center of trade, transport, and industry.

The town's center, as well as the harbor, was completely destroyed by German bombers on May 14, 1940. In the years following the war, every effort

ABOVE: Rotterdam is a large modern city and port. Much of it was bombed during the war but, fortunately, most of the center has now been reconstructed.

was made to reconstruct the city. In the 1960s, Rotterdam became the world's largest harbor; today, it is the largest in Europe. Meanwhile, a new city center was constructed with cosmopolitan appeal. This reconstruction has given Rotterdam its unique architectural character. A new inner city developed, with modern and functional architecture oriented toward the river, and a series of experiments in city planning have earned admiration from visitors from around the world.

ABOVE: *The Oudegracht Canal in the old center of Utrecht. The Dom Tower is in the background.*

Utrecht

Utrecht is almost 2,000 years old. It all began with a Roman fortification established in 47 BCE as part of the reinforcements along the river Rhine against invasions from Germania. In 1122 CE, Utrecht was granted a city charter, and the city's historic canals and wharves date from this period. For centuries, Utrecht was the only city of importance in the north of Holland, and it played a major role during the Eighty Years' War against Spain. In 1570, the famed Union of Utrecht was formed in the large chapter house, which is now the university auditorium. This was a beginning to the northern provinces' secession from Spanish rule, which led to the formation of the powerful Republic of the Seven United Netherlands, the first republic in postmedieval Europe. Additional growth came in 1636 with the founding of the university.

Text Dependent Questions

1. What is the capital city of the Netherlands?

2. What is the southernmost city in the Netherlands?

3. Where is the Dutch official seat of government?

Research Project

Find an image of one of the Dutch royal palaces, and then make a poster about it, advertising it to tourists.

Words to Understand

climate change: Changes in the Earth's weather patterns.

global warming: A warming of the earth's atmosphere and oceans that is thought to be a result of air pollution.

floodplains: Low, flat land along a stream that is flooded when the stream overflows.

BELOW: These floating houses in Houten, near Utrecht, have addressed the issue of flooding, for they can rise and fall with the water level.
.

Chapter Six
A BRIGHT FUTURE
FOR THE NETHERLANDS

The Netherlands is a low-lying nation. Only half of the country lies more than a meter above sea level, while an eighth of the country is below sea level. Without its network of dams, dikes, and dunes, the Netherlands would flood.

In the twenty-first century, the Netherlands faces a new challenge for the future: one of the predicted outcomes of global **climate change** is a rise in sea levels—and in the Netherlands, this could be devastating. That's why this nation is leading the world in its efforts to both fight and live with the changes brought about by **global warming**.

The Dutch people have been fighting the sea for thousands of years, first with artificial hills and then with stronger and bigger dikes. A special government think tank called the Delta Commissie has looked into three possible solutions to the dangers presented by global climate change: building a gigantic dam just off the coast in the North Sea; strengthening the existing dikes; and even evacuating the entire Dutch population to Germany. Climate-change expert Professor Pier Vellinga took part in the Delta Commissie; he warned, "If CO2 emissions aren't reduced the waters will ultimately rise more than 70 meters. Even the Dutch can't cope with that."

ABOVE: *Dutch and EU flags.*

But the Dutch are doing the best they can. As sea levels swell and storms become wilder, the Dutch are spending billions of euros on "floating communities" that can rise with surging flood waters, on enormous garages that double as urban **floodplains**, and on reengineering parts of the nation's coastline. The government is also relocating some farmers from flood-prone areas, and expanding rivers and canals to contain anticipated swells.

These measures are putting the Netherlands far ahead of the rest of the world in adapting to the climate changes that most scientists believe the entire Earth will eventually face. The Dutch have made adapting to global warming a

ABOVE: *The picturesque town of Haarlem. Like many Dutch towns and cities, it is in danger of flooding if sea levels rise.*

What is Global Climate Change—And Why are People So Worried About It?

Global climate change has to do with an average increase in the Earth's temperature. Most scientists agree that humans are responsible because of the pollution cars and factories have put into the air.

Global warming is already having serious impacts on humans and the environment in many ways. An increase in global temperatures causes rising sea levels (because of melting of the polar caps) and changes in the amount and pattern of precipitation. These changes may increase the frequency and intensity of extreme weather events, such as floods, droughts, heat waves, hurricanes, and tornadoes. Other consequences include changes to farms' crop production, species becoming extinct, and an increased spread of disease.

Not all experts agree about climate change, but almost all scientists believe that it is very real. Politicians and the public do not agree, though, on policies to deal with climate change. Changes in the way people live can be expensive, at both the personal and national levels, and not everyone is convinced that taking on these expenses needs to be a priority.

high priority for their nation. They know that the alternative could mean that in the years to come, they could lose their coastal cities altogether. Now the rest of the EU—and the rest of the world—will have to learn from their example.

The Environmental Policy in the Netherlands

The government of the Netherlands pursues a successful environmental policy that is resulting in cleaner rivers, a reduction in carbon emissions, a reduction in waste streams, and the cleanup of contaminated soil. There are still more challenges, including improving air quality, climate change, and the depletion of natural resources and biodiversity. National environmental policy is aimed at contributing to sustainable economic development and to the health and safety of the people by maintaining and improving the quality of the environment. The government is committed to sustainable management of the environment in the Netherlands and in the wider EU and global context.

However, environmental challenges will always present themselves, for the Netherlands is a highly populous and highly industrialized, the main areas of

ABOVE: *These modern houses have been fitted with solar panels, which generate clean renewable electricity for the residents.*

ABOVE: *The primary function of sea dikes is to protect low-lying coastal areas from flooding by the sea.*

ABOVE: *The Dutch are a happy, well-educated, very liberal nation who are tolerant and accepting of nearly everything.*

activity being petroleum, aircraft, food processing, chemicals, electronics and machinery. Agriculture is highly intensive and dairy farming is especially important. All these activities are at odds with the environment, so the government must work hard to counteract any damage to the environment that they make.

ABOVE: *A wind farm under construction. Even though the Dutch are working hard to increase renewable energy production, like many countries, they still have a way to go.*

Text Dependent Questions

1. What is the Delta Commissie?

2. What is a "floating community"?

3. Why are some Dutch farmers relocating to other areas?

Research Project

Is climate change man-made? What evidence is there that humans are causing it?

4100 BCE	Dolmens erected by prehistoric inhabitants of Dutch territory.
600	Germanic tribes occupy the area.
100 CE	Romans establish control over the region, which they name Germania Minor.
496	Franks gain control of Dutch territory and begin to convert the people to Christianity.
962	The Holy Roman Empire is established.
1548	Habsburg ruler Charles V grants the "Pragmatic Sanction" granting the Netherlands a measure of autonomy.
1568	The Eighty Years' War begins.
1579	The Republic of the Seven United Netherlands is formed.
1602	The Dutch East India Company is incorporated.
1648	The Eighty Years' War ends, and the republic is granted independence.
1795	Napoleon invades the Netherlands.
1815	The Dutch monarchy is established.
1848	The Netherlands becomes a constitutional monarchy.
1914	World War I begins; the Netherlands remains neutral.
1922	Women are granted the right to vote.
1940	Nazi Germany invades the Netherlands.
1944	Operation Market Garden liberates the southern portion of the country.
1945	The Allies liberate the rest of the country from the Nazis.
1945	The Netherlands becomes a charter member of the United Nations.
1949	The Netherlands becomes a founding member of NATO.
1957	The European Economic Community begins between Germany, France, Belgium, Italy, Luxembourg, and the Netherlands.
1992	The Maastricht Treaty is signed, creating the EU.
2002	The Netherlands adopts the euro.
2008	The world enters a global recession.
2010	The Netherlands begins to emerge from the recession.
2012	Liberals and Labour form a coalition headed by Mark Rutte. The new government warns that tough austerity measures will be needed.
2013	Willem-Alexander becomes king.
2014	Malaysian Airlines flight MH17 travelling from Amsterdam to Kuala Lumpur crashes in eastern Ukraine, close to the border with Russia.
2017	Prime Minister Mark Rutte forms a coalition after a record 225 days of talks following elections in March.

Further Reading

Harmans, Gerard M. L. *DK Eyewitness Travel Guide*: The Netherlands. London: DK, 2017.

McCormick, John. *Understanding the European Union: A Concise Introduction*. London: Palgrave Macmillan, 2017.

Mason, David S. *A Concise History of Modern Europe: Liberty, Equality, Solidarity*. London: Rowman & Littlefield, 2015.

Steves, Rick. Openshaw, Gene. *Rick Steves Amsterdam & the Netherlands*. Edmonds: Rick Steves' Europe, Inc., 2017.

Internet Resources

The Netherlands Travel Information and Travel Guide
www.lonelyplanet.com/the-netherlands

The Netherlands Tourism Guide
http://www.netherlands-tourism.com

The Netherlands: Country Profile
http://www.bbc.co.uk/news/world-europe-17740800

The Netherlands: CIA World Factbook
https://www.cia.gov/library/publications/the-world-factbook/geos/nl.html

The Official Website of the European Union
europa.eu/index_en.htm

Publisher's note:
The websites listed on this page were active at the time of publication. The publisher is not responsible for websites that have changed their addressees or discontinued operation since the date of publication. The publisher will review and update the website list upon each reprint.

Author

Dominic J. Ainsley is a freelance writer on history, geography, and the arts and the author of many books on travel. His passion for traveling dates from when he visited Europe at the age of ten with his parents. Today, Dominic travels the world for work and pleasure, documenting his experiences and encounters as he goes. He lives in the south of England in the United Kingdom with his wife and two children.